# Greatest Heroes and Legends OF THE BIBLE

# The Easter Story

## retold by K.S. Rodriguez & Mary Hogan
## illustrated by Jan Gregg-Kelm

inchworm PRESS
TM

    A festival is held every year in Jerusalem to celebrate Passover. At Passover, Jewish people remember the time that God freed them from slavery in Egypt.

    Two thousand years ago, Jesus was one of the people traveling to Jerusalem to celebrate this holiday. Jesus traveled with twelve of his closest followers: Simon Peter, Andrew, James, John, Philip, Bartholomew, Thomas, Matthew, James, Thaddeus, Simon the Zealot, and Judas.

These followers were called disciples because they believed in the teachings of Jesus. Jesus called God his Father, and taught his disciples to do the same. He wanted everyone to love God above all else, and to show that love by treating each other with respect and caring.

When Jesus arrived in Jerusalem, a large crowd gathered to welcome him. The people layed palm leaves in front of his path as a sign of honor. "Blessed is he that comes in the name of the Lord!" shouted the people. Jesus went among them, healing the sick, the blind, the lame—and always praising God.

Some religious leaders watched the procession, regarding the crowd with fear and anger. They had heard of this man who claimed to the be the Son of God, and they didn't like how the people turned to Jesus instead of them.

Soon Jesus made the priests even angrier. When he walked into the temple, Jesus saw that the holy place had been turned into a marketplace. Merchants were buying and selling goods and animals in the space that should have been used for worshipping God!

Jesus shouted, "It is written, 'My house shall be called a house of prayer,' but you have turned it into a house of thieves!"

The high priest, Caiaphas, decided that Jesus was making too much trouble. It was time to get rid of Jesus for good.

The priests wanted to destroy Jesus, but they did not know how to find him—until a hooded man paid them a visit. "I understand that you seek Jesus of Nazareth," the man said. "I am in a position to deliver him to you." The man removed his hood. He was Judas, one of Jesus's own disciples!

Judas told the priests that he no longer believed that Jesus was the Son of God. The priests promised Judas thirty silver pieces if he would help them capture Jesus. Judas agreed.

The next day, Jesus and the twelve disciples gathered for the Passover meal. After they prayed together, Jesus announced, "I tell you before it happens that one of you will betray me."

The disciples were shocked! They demanded to know which of them would do such a thing. "He who eats bread with me is the one who will betray me," he said. Jesus dipped a piece of bread into a bowl. Then he held out the bread to Judas.

When Judas took the bread, Jesus whispered to him, "That which you do, do quickly." Judas grew fearful and ran from the table!

Jesus shared the rest of the bread with the remaining followers. "Take and eat," he said. "For this is my body which is given for you. Do this in remembrance of me."

Then Jesus filled his cup with wine. "Drink, for this is my blood shed for the forgiveness of sins." He passed the cup to his disciples.

When the feast was finished, it was nightfall. Jesus and the disciples went to a place called Gethsemane to pray.

As they sat around the campfire, Jesus put his hand on Simon Peter's shoulder and told him, "I tell you that this night, before the cock crows, you will deny me three times."

Simon Peter was upset by the prophecy. "No, Lord," he said. "I would gladly die with you. I won't ever deny you!" The others joined in, agreeing that they, too, would never deny him. But instead of keeping watch over their teacher, every last one fell asleep.

Jesus knew his hour had come. He prayed, "O my Father, if it be possible, let this cup pass from me."

Suddenly, a hand grabbed Jesus by the shoulder! Judas faced Jesus, saying, "Hail, Master." He leaned in and kissed Jesus on the cheek.

"Judas, do you betray the Son of God with a kiss?" Jesus asked.

Before Judas could answer, Jesus was surrounded by soldiers with drawn swords! Judas had told them that the man that he kissed was the one they should capture. "Arrest this man!" their captain called out.

The disciples fled into the woods to avoid capture. And when asked if he was Jesus's follower, Simon Peter denied it three times.

Jesus was taken before Caiaphas and the other religious leaders and placed on trial. The priests were certain that the claim of a poor preacher to be the Son of God was a lie, and an insult to the Jewish religion.

Caiaphas asked Jesus, "Do you claim to be the Messiah, the Son of God?"

Jesus answered, "I am . . . as you say."
Before the people and the court, Jesus had willingly incriminated himself.
The judges quickly ruled that Jesus should be punished and they sentenced
him to death.

The soldiers beat and taunted Jesus as they dragged him through the streets. "If you're really who you say you are, why don't you summon an army of angels to save you?"

Judas watched the soldiers torture Jesus and was overwhelmed with guilt. He realized that Jesus would be put to death because of his betrayal. In despair, Judas hung himself.

Next, Jesus was taken before the Roman governor, Pontius Pilate, who had the authority to carry out the sentence of death. Pontius Pilate did not want to be involved with a religious dispute. He asked the crowd to choose between Jesus and another prisoner: who should be punished and who should be set free.

The crowd shouted for Jesus to be punished. "Crucify him!" they shouted.

The soldiers placed a thorny crown on Jesus's head. Then they made him carry his own cross to his crucifixion.

At the top of a rocky hill called "The Skull," the soldiers nailed Jesus to the cross. "Father, why have you forsaken me?" cried Jesus.

A storm broke in Jerusalem and an earthquake shook the land. The great, thick veil that hung in the Temple split down the center.

"Father, I give my spirit up into Your hands," said Jesus. And then he died.

Jesus's body was placed in a tomb, which was tightly sealed by a boulder. Mary Magdalene and Mary, mother of James, were two followers of Jesus who came to the tomb every day to pray. On the third day after Jesus's death, the two women found that the tomb was open. The boulder was rolled aside, and an angel stood inside.

The angel rejoiced, "Tell it from Jerusalem to Galilee. Tell the disciples. Christ is risen!"

Mary Magdalene and Mary were overjoyed! But when they told the disciples what they had seen, the men did not believe them.

Finally all the disciples gathered in Galilee and Jesus himself appeared to them. "Peace be with you," he said.

"My lord, is it really you?" asked Simon Peter.

"Yes," said Jesus. "I died for the sins of all people—so that you might know salvation and eternal life in the kingdom of God. As my Father sent me, so I send you. Go, and teach all nations to respect my teachings."

Jesus appeared among the disciples for forty days. On the fortieth day, he said, "Remember that I am always with you." And with that, he rose up before the disciples and ascended into heaven.

The disciples were filled with happiness. They went throughout the world, spreading the Good News that Jesus had risen, teaching people everywhere his lessons of love and faith.